Hansel and Gretel

Hansel and Gretel

BY THE BROTHERS GRIMM

TRANSLATED BY CHARLES SCRIBNER, JR.

ILLUSTRATED BY

ADRIENNE ADAMS

CHARLES SCRIBNER'S SONS
NEW YORK

To Lisa Damon

A poor woodcutter once lived by the edge of a forest with his two children and their stepmother. The little boy's name was Hansel and the little girl's name was Gretel. The family never had much to eat and, once, when there was a terrible famine throughout the land, they were all close to starving.

One night as the woodcutter was worrying about his problems and tossing and turning on his bed, he gave a great sigh and said to his wife, "What is going to become of us? How are we going to feed our poor children when we have nothing more to eat ourselves?"

"I know what we'll do," replied his wife. "Very early tomorrow morning we'll take the children out into the thickest part of the forest and there we'll light a fire for them and give them each a piece of bread. Then we'll go back to our work and leave them by themselves. They will never find their way home, and so we'll be rid of them."

"No, wife," said the woodcutter, "I won't do such a thing! How could I ever bring myself to leave my children alone in the forest? Wild animals would come and tear them to pieces."

"Oh, you fool!" she said. "In that case all four of us will have to starve to death." And she gave him no peace until he finally gave in.

"But I'm still unhappy about the poor children," said her husband.

The two children had not been able to get to sleep either, because they were so hungry. And so they heard what their stepmother suggested to their father. Gretel wept bitterly and said to Hansel, "Now we are done for."

"Be quiet, Gretel," said Hansel, "and don't be afraid. I'll take good care of us."

And when the grown-ups had gone to sleep, he got up, put on his jacket, opened the lower part of the door, and slipped out. The moon was shining brightly and the white pebbles that lay in front of the house shone like coins of pure silver. Hansel bent down and stuffed as many of them as he could into his jacket pocket. Then he went back in and said to Gretel, "Cheer up, sister dear. Now you can sleep peacefully. God will not forsake us." And he went back to bed.

At daybreak their stepmother came in and awakened the two children: "Get up, you lazybones, we are going to go into the forest to gather wood."

She gave each of them a piece of bread and said, "There's something for your lunch, but don't eat it before then. You won't be getting anything more."

Gretel put the bread in her apron because Hansel had the stones in his pocket. Then they all set out together for the forest. When they had gone a little way, Hansel stood still and looked back toward the house. He kept doing that, again and again. His father said, "Hansel, what are you looking at, and why are you falling behind? Pay attention and get a move on."

"Oh, Father," said Hansel, "I am looking at my little white cat, which is sitting up on the roof. It wants to say good-bye to me."

His stepmother said, "You fool, that is not your little cat, that is only the morning sun shining on the chimney." But Hansel really was not looking at the little cat at all. He was throwing the white pebbles from his pocket down on the path, one after another.

When they had come to the middle of the forest, their father said, "Now children, start picking up wood and I'll light a fire so you won't freeze."

Hansel and Gretel made a pile of brushwood as high as a small mountain. The brushwood was set on fire and when the flames were rising really high, their stepmother said, "Now children, go lie down by the fire and rest yourselves. We are going off to cut wood. When we are finished, we'll come back for you."

Hansel and Gretel sat by the fire, and when noon came, they both ate their piece of bread. Because they kept hearing the blows of the ax they believed that their father was still nearby. But actually it was not his ax at all. It was only a branch he had fastened to a dead tree that was being blown back and forth by the wind. When the children had sat there a long while, they became so tired that they could not keep their eyes open and they fell fast asleep. When they finally woke up it was pitch-dark. Gretel began to cry and said, "Now how will we ever get out of the forest?"

But Hansel cheered her up: "Just wait until the moon comes up and then we'll find our way home all right." And when the full moon had risen, Hansel took his little sister by the hand and followed the pebbles that glittered like brand-new coins in the moonlight and showed them the way.

They walked all through the night, and at daybreak they were back at their father's house. They knocked on the door, and when their stepmother opened it and saw that it was Hansel and Gretel, she cried, "You bad children, why did you sleep so long in the forest? We thought you would never come back."

But their father was joyful, for he had been heartbroken to have left them behind all by themselves.

Not long afterward there was another great famine throughout the land, and the children heard their stepmother saying to their father in bed: "Everything has been eaten up. We now have only half a loaf of bread. When that is gone, we're finished. The children will have to go. We'll take them even deeper into the forest this time so they'll never find their way back. Otherwise nothing can save us."

This almost broke her husband's heart, and he said to himself: "It would be better if we shared our last morsel with our children." But his wife would not listen to any of his pleas. Now he who says A must also say B, and because he had given in the first time he had to do so the second time, too.

The children were still awake and overheard all this. So when the grown-ups were asleep, Hansel got up to go out and pick up some pebbles as he had done the time before. But their stepmother had locked the door. He still comforted his little sister though and said to her, "Don't cry, Gretel, and sleep peacefully. The good Lord will surely help us."

Early the next morning their stepmother came in and got the children out of bed. She gave them each a piece of bread. It was even smaller this time than the last time. On the way into the forest Hansel crumbled the bread in his pocket, and he would stop every so often and drop a little piece on the ground.

"Hansel, why are you standing there? What are you staring at?" asked his father. "Keep going."

"I am looking at my little dove, which is sitting on the roof," answered Hansel. "It wants to say good-bye to me."

"You fool," said his stepmother. "That is only the morning sun that is shining on top of the chimney."

But Hansel kept dropping little pieces of bread along the way, one after another.

The stepmother led the children deeper and deeper into the forest until they reached a place they had never been before in their whole life. There they lighted a huge fire again, and their stepmother said, "Sit down there, children, and don't go away. If you get tired you can sleep a little. We are going off to cut wood, and in the evening when we are finished we'll come and get you."

When noon came, Gretel gave some of her bread to Hansel, because he had scattered his own bread along the way. Then they went to sleep until the evening. No one came for the poor children, and it was pitch-dark when they woke up. Hansel comforted his little sister and said, "Just wait until the moon rises. Then we will see the bread crumbs which I have scattered and they will show us the way home."

When the moon rose they got up, but they couldn't find a single crumb, because the thousands of birds that fly back and forth in the meadow and the forest had picked them all up.

Hansel said to Gretel, "Surely we'll find our way." But they did not find it. They walked the whole night long and then another whole day from morning to evening, but they still could not find their way out of the woods. They were now very hungry, for they had had nothing to eat except for a few berries which they had found lying on the ground. When they were so tired that they could not drag their legs any farther, they lay down under a tree and went to sleep.

It was now the third morning since they had left their father's house. They started on their way again, but they went deeper and deeper into the forest. If help did not come soon they were certainly

going to die. At noontime, they saw a beautiful little snow-white bird sitting on a branch. It sang so beautifully that they stood still and listened to it. When it had finished its song, it flapped its wings and flew off in front of them. They followed it until they were brought to a little house. There the bird perched on the roof. When the children came up close they saw that the little house was made out of bread and was covered with cookies. The windows were made out of clear sugar.

"Here is where we ought to pitch right in," said Hansel, "and have ourselves a good meal. I'll eat a piece of the roof, Gretel, and you can eat some of the window. The window will taste sweet." Then Hansel reached up and broke off a bit of the roof to see how it would taste, and Gretel stood in front of the windowpanes and started to break one of them. All at once a squeaky voice called out from the room inside:

> *A tap, a rap, a tap again.*
> *Who's tapping on my windowpane?*

The children answered:

> *It's the wind that's so wild.*
> *It's the heavens' own child.*

And they kept right on eating without looking up. Hansel liked the taste of the roof very much and tore down a great piece of it for himself. And Gretel knocked out a whole round windowpane. Then suddenly the door opened and an old woman, as old as the hills, hobbled out, leaning on a crutch.

Hansel and Gretel were terribly frightened and they dropped what they held in their hands. But the old woman wagged her head to and fro and said, "Ah, ha! You dear little children, who has brought you here? Just come right in and stay with me. No harm will come to you." She took them both by the hand and led them into her little house. There she brought out a delicious meal of pancakes with sugar and apples and nuts. After that she put white sheets on two beautiful little beds. Hansel and Gretel lay down in them and thought they were in heaven.

But the old woman had only pretended to be so friendly. She was really a wicked witch who lay in wait for children. She had built the little bread house simply to lure them to her. Whenever one of them came into her power she killed it, cooked it, and ate it. That was a feast day for her!

Witches have red eyes and cannot see very far, but they have a fantastic sense of smell, just as animals have. In that way they can tell when people are coming near. When Hansel and Gretel were coming toward her house the wicked witch had laughed to herself and said mockingly: "I've got them now. They'll never be able to get away from me."

Early in the morning, before the children were awake, she was up already. When she saw the two of them lying there so sweetly, with their plump, red cheeks, she cackled to herself: "That will be a tasty mouthful."

Then she seized Hansel with her skinny hands and dragged him into a little shed and locked him in with a door made of iron bars. He could scream as loud as he pleased but it would not help him any.

Then she went to Gretel and shook her until she was awake. "Get up, you lazy girl," she shouted. "Go get some water and cook something good for your brother. He is sitting outside in the shed and has to be fattened up. When he's fat enough I am going to eat him." Gretel began to weep bitterly but it was all in vain. She had to do what the wicked witch told her to.

And so all the best food was cooked for poor Hansel, while Gretel got nothing to eat except crab-shells. Each morning the old woman would hobble out to the little shed and cry, "Hansel, stick out your finger so I can feel whether you are getting fat." But Hansel would stick out a little bone. The old woman had very weak eyes and could not see the bone. So she thought it was Hansel's finger and wondered why he never got any fatter.

When four weeks had passed and Hansel still stayed thin, her impatience got the better of her and she did not want to wait any longer. "Hey there, Gretel!" she shouted to the little girl. "Step lively and fetch some water. Hansel may be fat or he may be thin, but tomorrow I am going to butcher him and eat him."

Alas, how the poor little sister wept and wailed when she had to fetch the water. "Dear God, help us, please!" she cried out. "If

only the wild beasts in the forest had eaten us up. Then at least we could both have died together."

"Stop your whining," said the old woman. "It won't help you a bit."

Early the next morning Gretel was forced to hang up the kettle of water and light the fire. "First we're going to bake," said the old woman. "I have heated the oven already and I have kneaded the dough." She pushed poor Gretel out toward the oven. Fiery flames were streaming out of it now.

"Crawl in," said the witch, "and see whether it is hot enough for us to put in the bread." Once Gretel was in there, the witch was going to shut the oven, so that Gretel would be baked in it. Then she was going to eat her, too.

But Gretel saw what she was planning to do and said, "I don't know how I'm going to do that. How can I get in there?"

"You silly goose," said the old woman, "the opening is plenty big enough. Watch this, I could get in there myself." And she hobbled up to it and stuck her head inside the oven.

Then Gretel gave her a great big shove and pushed her all the way in. She closed the iron door and fastened the bolt. My, how the witch began to howl. It was really gruesome! But Gretel ran away, and left the wicked witch to be burned to a cinder.

Gretel ran straight to Hansel. She opened the little shed and shouted, "Hansel, we are saved. The old witch is dead."

When the door was opened for him, Hansel leaped out, like a bird from a cage. The two children threw their arms around each other and danced for joy. They did not need to be afraid anymore so they went into the witch's house. In every corner of it there were chests filled with pearls and precious stones.

"These are even better than the pebbles," said Hansel, putting as many as he could into his pocket.

Gretel said, "I will take some home, too." And she filled her apron with them.

"Now we'll have to be on our way," said Hansel, "if we are ever going to get out of the witch's forest."

When they had been walking for a couple of hours they came upon a wide river. "We can't cross over this," said Hansel. "I don't see a bridge or even a plank to cross on."

"There are no ferryboats either," said Gretel. "But I see a white duck swimming there. If I ask it to, it will help us across." Then she called,

> Oh, little duck! Oh, little duck!
> The two of us are out of luck.
> No bridge, no plank. Alas, alack.
> Won't you take us on your back?

The little duck came over, and Hansel sat on its back and told his sister to get on, too.

"No," replied Gretel, "it would be too heavy for the little duck. It will have to take us over one at a time."

The little duck did just that, and when they were safely on

the other side and had gone a little farther, the forest began to look more and more familiar to them.

At last they caught a glimpse of their father's house far ahead. Then they began to run. They burst into the room and threw their arms around their father's neck. That man had not spent a happy hour since he had left the children in the forest. His wife was dead now.

Gretel shook out her apron so that the pearls and precious stones scattered all over the floor. Then Hansel threw handfuls of them out of his pocket. And so all their troubles were over at last, and they lived together in perfect happiness.

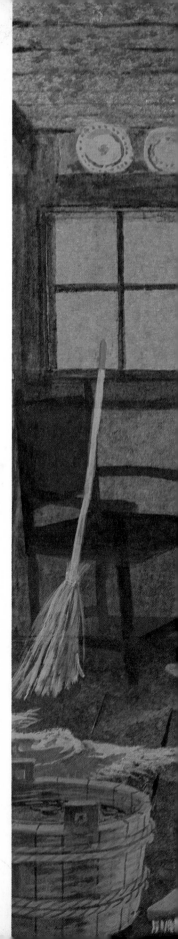

My story is done,
See the mouse run.
If it's caught in a trap,
You can make a fur cap.

DATE DUE

OCT 7 '76			
OCT 1 4 '76			
SEP 2 1 '77			
DEC 6 '77			
F			
Hinton			
FEB 26 '80			
Judd			
MAY 05 '81			
SEP 17 '82			
Klotz			
MAY 22 '84			
MAY 26 '84			
MAY 08 1985			
NOV 14 1985			
3-20-90			
GAYLORD			PRINTED IN U S A